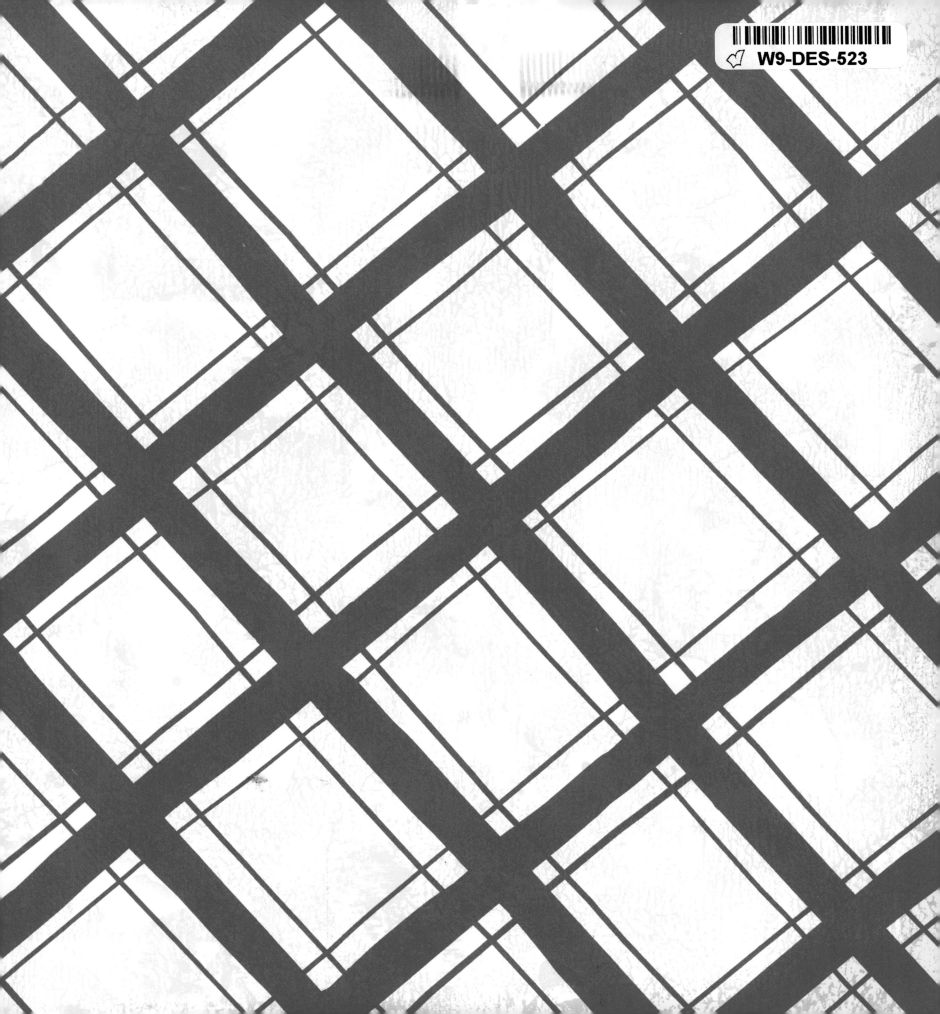

PICK,
PECK through the top.
Push,
poke,
out I POP!

Pauline
Poulet

Growing, growing,
chick to hen.
I cluck triumphant,
CLUCK AGAIN!

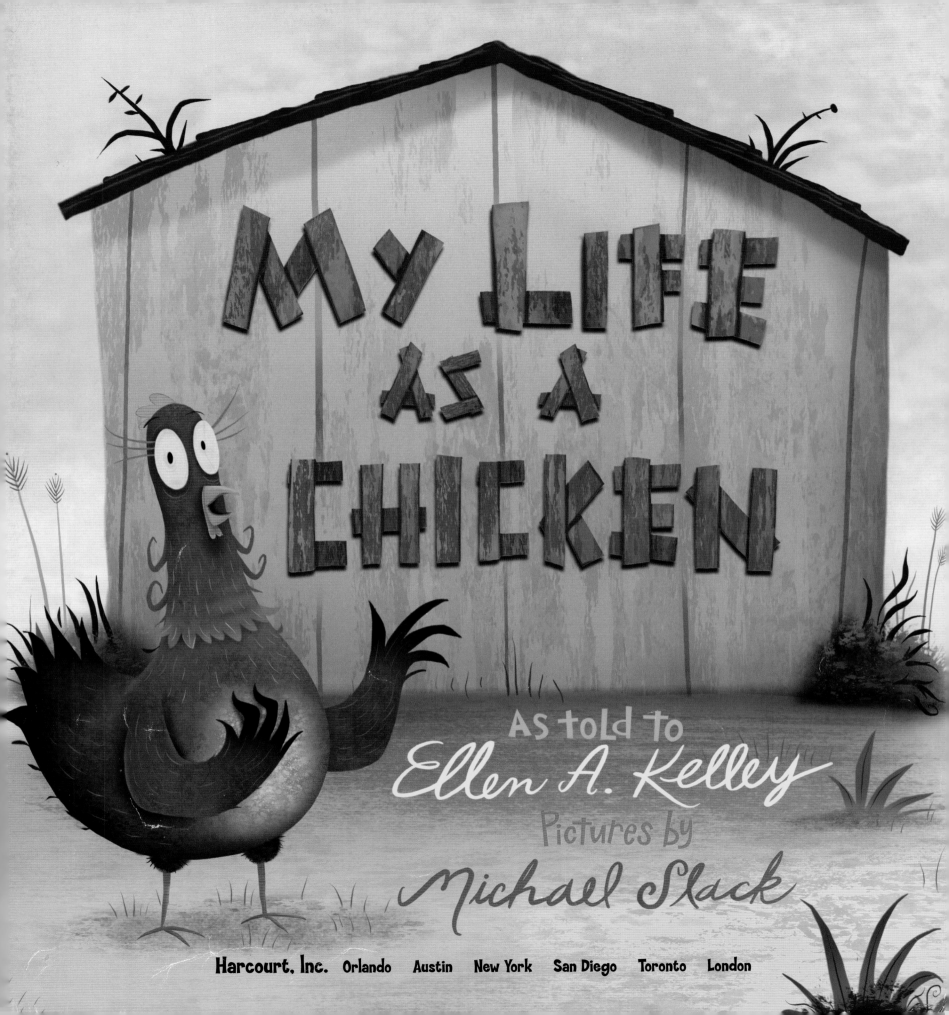

My Life as a Chicken

As told to
Ellen A. Kelley

Pictures by
Michael Slack

Harcourt, Inc.   Orlando   Austin   New York   San Diego   Toronto   London www.HarcourtBooks.com

Library of Congress Cataloging-in-Publication Data
Kelley, Ellen A.
My life as a chicken/Ellen A. Kelley; illustrated by Michael Slack.
p.   cm.
Summary: After escaping the frying pan, a chicken has an adventure that includes
pirates, a typhoon, and a balloon ride before landing happily in a petting zoo.
[1. Chickens—Fiction.   2. Adventure and adventurers—Fiction.
3. Stories in rhyme.]   I. Slack, Michael H., 1969- ill.   II. Title.
PZ8.3.K338Myal   2007
[E]—dc22   2005020051
ISBN 978-0-15-205306-2

First edition
H G F E D C B A

Manufactured in China

The illustrations in this book were done digitally using mixed media.
The display lettering was created by Michael Slack.
The text type was set in Coop and Potato Cut.
Color separations by Bright Arts Ltd., Hong Kong
Manufactured by South China Printing Company, Ltd., China
This book was printed on totally chlorine-free Stora Enso Matte paper.
Production supervision by Pascha Gerlinger
Designed by Lauren Rille

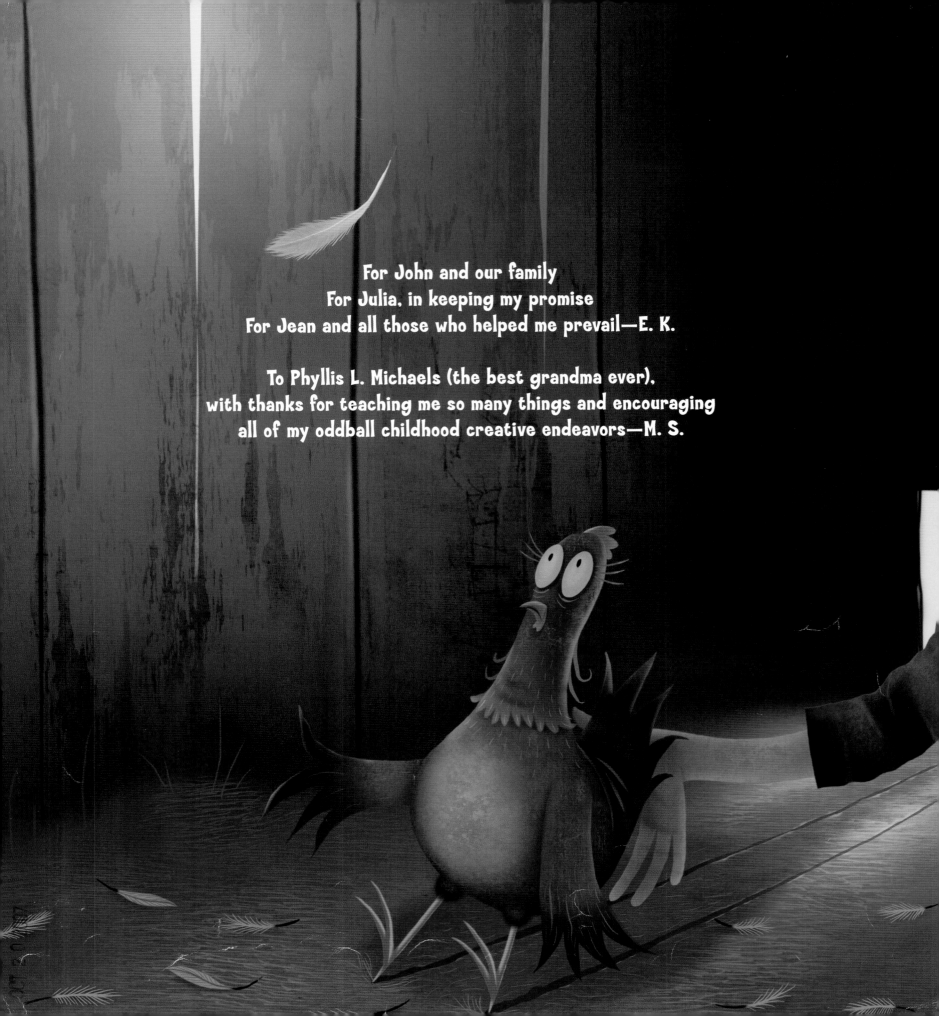

For John and our family
For Julia, in keeping my promise
For Jean and all those who helped me prevail—E. K.

To Phyllis L. Michaels (the best grandma ever),
with thanks for teaching me so many things and encouraging
all of my oddball childhood creative endeavors—M. S.

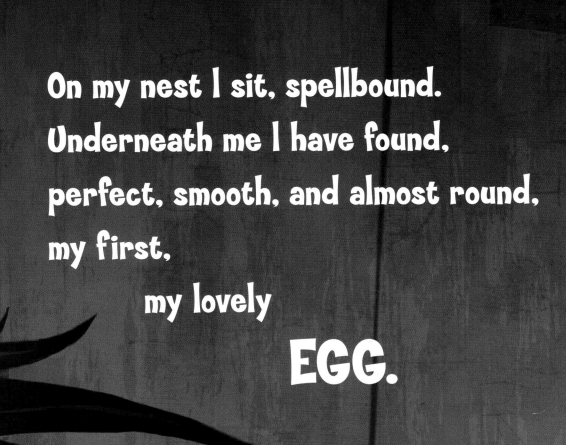

On my nest I sit, spellbound.
Underneath me I have found,
perfect, smooth, and almost round,
my first,

my lovely

EGG.

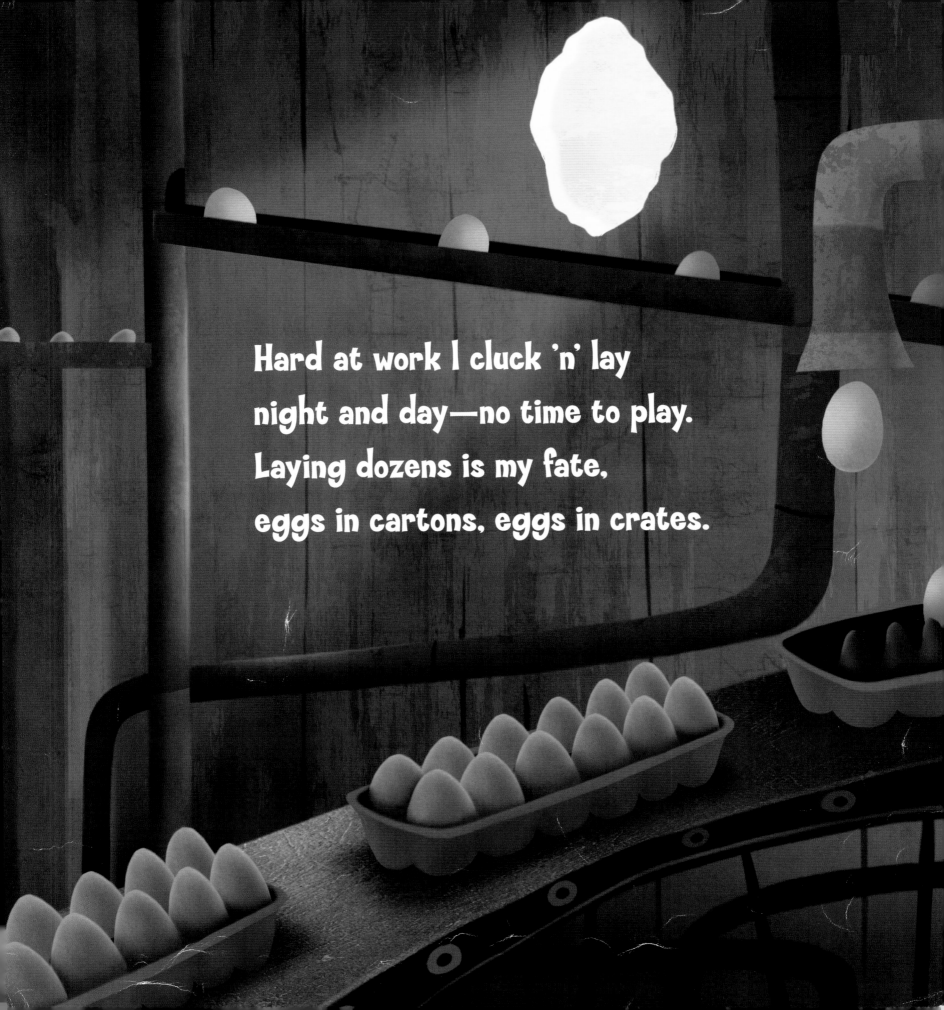

Hard at work I cluck 'n' lay
night and day—no time to play.
Laying dozens is my fate,
eggs in cartons, eggs in crates.

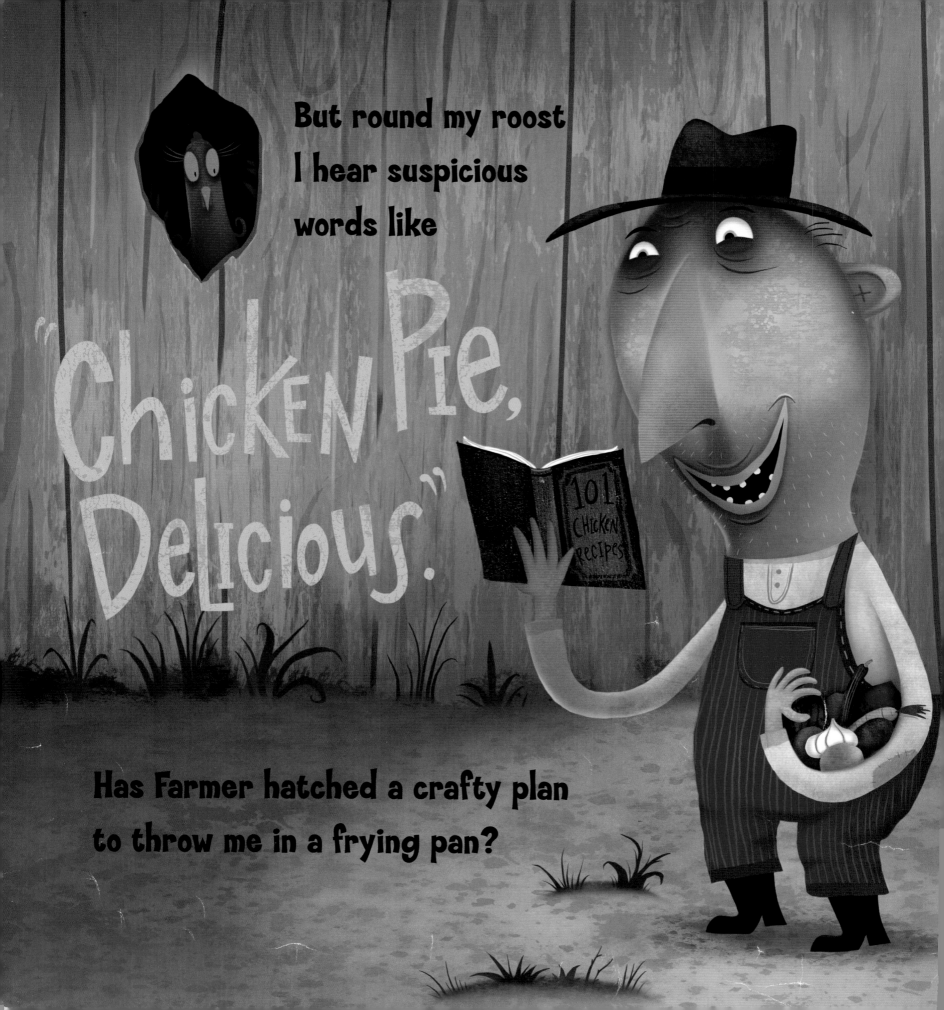

But round my roost
I hear suspicious
words like

"Chicken Pie,
Delicious."

Has Farmer hatched a crafty plan
to throw me in a frying pan?

I'll be his special of the day
at Cock-a-Doodle-Doo Café!

BAWWWK!

HENS, AWAY!

Out the gate,
I must escape
the dinner plate!

To the brooding woods I scramble,
prickly briar'd, bristly brambled.
I am chased by hungry brutes.
I am spooked by swoopy hoots.

I squeeze inside a log to hide.
Fox is mad. He's stuck outside.
He snarls and snaps.
I flinch and flail,
then raise my cry,

"Pauline,
Prevail!"

Now a windy whip-and-twirl
sucks us up inside its swirl,
then spits us out:
Fox, log, and me.

I tumble to
CataStRophe.

...to the sea, dunked and washed,
almost drowned, soppy-sloshed.

Then pirates pull me
from the foam.

Why, oh why,
did I leave home?

I polish brass and sweep the scupper,
but Captain wants me for his supper.
The ship's cook reaches for my neck!
I flap fast past the quarterdeck.

By sneaking off this shifty ship,
I'll give these scalawags the slip.
Hours pass atop the mast.
I wait.
The sea cats snooze at last!

Yawn

I tiptoe aft, steal a raft,
brave the waves,
and sail my craft.

I face the fearsome typhoon's wail, clucking loud,

"Pauline, Prevail!"

I am tossed, tail over beak,
landing hard, a wet-hen heap,
in something bobbing on the tide:
a basket—dry, unoccupied.

WHAT NOW?

A pull, a lift, surprising!

From the water I am rising,

crossing sea, skimming moon,

carried by a big balloon.

I navigate high altitudes,

an aeronaut with fortitude.

Above me burns a blaze of stars,

below the view blurs fast and far.

One hen aloft, so all alone–

WiLL I ever
find A home?

From the corner of my eye,
I spy a speck high in the sky.
It circles closer, then arrives—

A HAWK!

I duck.
Claws out, it dives.

I hear a hiss, a pop.
I'm dropping—
plummeting to earth,
no stopping!
From the basket's rail,
I bail.
"Be brave!" I cluck.

"Pauline,
Prevail!"

Then coming fast,
hard on the right,
I see a paper bird.
A kite!
We meet.
I leap and latch on tight.

I ride the kite,

cling and swing,

wilted, wounded,
weak of wing,

then fall, crashing hard and steep,
deep into chicken sleep.

Whispers wake me, gentle, shy.
Cradled, smoothed, and soothed am I,
carried somewhere safe and warm:
a soft straw bed near coops of corn.

Neighbors with the goats and sheep,
piglets, ducklings, chicks who peep,

I've found a paradise for me:
new friends, new nest, new family.
My new home is this petting zoo.

I think I'll stay.

Now, wouldn't you?

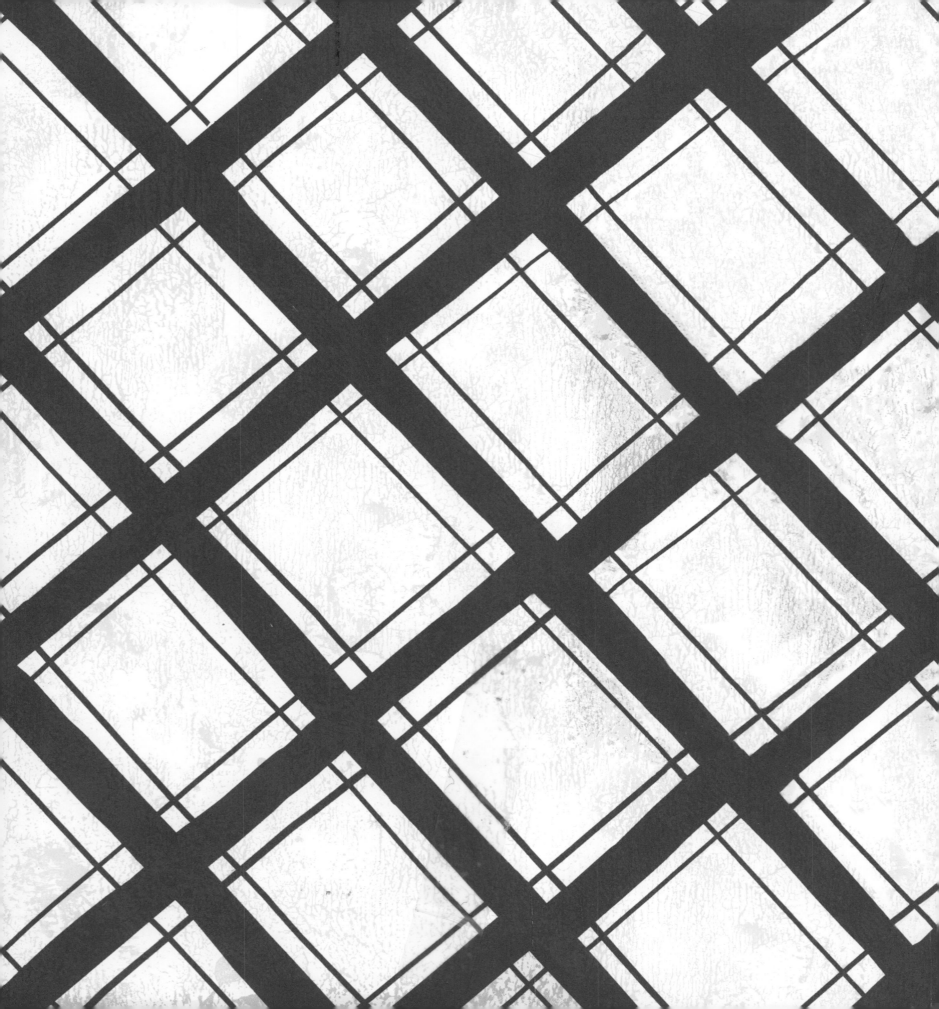